HEART OF FLAME

ROXIE CLARKE

WRITE
FREE
PRESS

$\mathcal{B}$ea plated up another five pieces of the vanilla sheet cake with champagne filling onto the white dessert plates. She would serve these alongside the small, fancy wedding cake reserved for the bride and groom.

While most of the other wedding guests were out on the dance floor cheering on an older couple kissing under the Mistletoe Cactus, Bea preferred to work. Normally, she liked to have a project to keep her hands busy, but today especially, she was full of nervous energy.

Going on two years sober, this was the first large-scale celebration she'd attended.

Mojo beers from the brewpub next door to the Pinwheel Plant Shop, where she worked part-time, were being served as well as their draft root beer and cream soda.

She wasn't worried she would somehow take a drink of beer and end up blackout drunk on the dance floor doing a striptease—Bea was done with that level of idiocy—but she still had cravings from time-to-time to just relax with a beer or a glass of wine to calm her nerves.

That was what made her other part-time job as a server at The Headless Horseman pub a nightmare. The lure to stay after work with the other servers and bartenders, to have a drink or six to wind down from the day, had taken its toll on her well-being.

When her manager at the Pinwheel, Layla, was able to give her five additional hours a week at the beginning of December, Bea had quit the Horseman. However, what was good for her soul was trash for her budget.

Her January rent was due in a little over a week and for the first time in a long time, Bea was going to come up short. She'd shared the two-bedroom apartment with her boyfriend, Chris, but when Bea quit drinking, he hadn't wanted to and bailed on her. It had been tough, but Bea had managed to work enough hours at multiple part-time jobs to afford rent on her own.

Bea had looked into downsizing to a one-bedroom or even a studio, but none were available in her apartment complex and moving to another complex meant paying first and last month's rent plus a cleaning deposit. So, she had to get a roommate. There was no way around it.

Good thing it was the end of December and had just snowed a foot. People were looking to move this time of year, weren't they?

Bea sighed, kept her head down, and moved on to plating up the chocolate sheet cake with raspberry filling.

❧

"What can I pour for you?" Lewis asked from behind the table he was using as a bar, working to keep his voice at a personable level. "I've got Mojo IPA, Braverton Blonde and Old Town Stout for the beer choices. Draft root beer and cream soda, made in house, for non-alcoholic choices."

He smiled at the woman, his eyebrows raised, waiting for her decision. Was that a brief look of shock he detected passing over her features? After his most recent argument with his ex-girlfriend and somehow still current roommate, Simone, he was feeling insecure.

"Wow," the woman said. "Your voice is really low." She snorted. "I'm sure you haven't heard that before."

"Never," Lewis said, allowing what he liked to think of as his *business grin* to pull the corners of his mouth up. "What'll it be?"

"I'll take a blonde and a stout for my boyfriend," she said, leaning toward Lewis and whispering, "he's the one responsible for the helicopter."

Lewis nodded, genuinely impressed. The groom's entrance had been epic. "Cool," he said, pouring their beers from the pony kegs set up on a table behind him. "That makes you Layla from the plant shop, then, correct?"

"Yes," she said. "My, how word gets around."

Lewis could tell she loved that it did, and he softened toward her some. He was feeling grumpy being around all this love when he was tragically single.

"And you are?" she asked.

"Lewis Tryon," he said, setting the beers on the table in front of her. "I just started as a craft brewer at Mojo in October. Hence why I'm slinging drinks while my mentor, Arthur, is dancing horribly with his wife out on the dance floor."

"Ah-ha," Layla said, laughing. "I thought you looked vaguely familiar. Like I'd seen you in the parking lot behind the Pinwheel. It's nice to meet you officially, Lewis." She picked up the beers and started to leave, then turned back. "Are you by any chance an untethered entity?"

Lewis chuckled. "If you're asking if I'm single, the answer is yes."

"Oh, good. Could you do me a favor?" she asked.

"Sure," Lewis said, wondering what she was getting at.

"See that redhead over there going to

town plating up cake?" she said, nodding in the redhead's direction.

"Uh-huh," Lewis said.

"Will you take her a root beer and tell her I said it's time for a break?"

"Okay," Lewis said. "Or I could pour a root beer for you to—"

"Thanks!" Layla said, turning and rushing away from him.

Lewis helped three more people before he had a lull. He poured a root beer, a cream soda, and a blonde to be on the safe side. People deserved choices.

He carried two drinks in the palm of one hand and one in the other. His large hands and years of experience as a server during college allowed him to hold the glasses this way.

Lewis approached the cake table and set the drinks down one by one.

"You can't put those there," the redhead said. "They're going to cut the cake soon and then people will get their slices from here and if your three drinks are there someone is bound to knock one over." She glared at the glasses. "Why in the world do you have three drinks?"

Lewis stood up straight and put his shoulders back. He was at least a foot taller than this cute little nippy dog of a woman. "These drinks are for you," he said, not holding back and using his full, deeper than deep voice. "Layla asked me to bring them over and to tell you it's time for a break."

"Layla told you to bring me a beer?" the redhead asked, using her index finger to push the glass of blonde away from her.

"Well, no," Lewis said. "She told me root beer, but I thought you'd like to choose for yourself."

"Oh, okay," she said, lifting the glass of root beer to her lips and taking a sip. "I don't drink alcohol and I prefer the root beer over the cream soda. Layla picked right."

Lewis nodded and picked up the discarded drinks. "Guess I'll have to drink both of these then." He held the glasses up to the light. "How'd you know one was beer and the other soda? They look almost identical." *To a laywoman's eye.*

"I can smell the difference," she said. "I was a server at The Headless Horseman for a while."

He took a drink of the blonde. It was a

perfect specimen if he did say so himself. "I haven't been to that pub yet," he said. "Since I started at Mojo I've been eating, sleeping, and breathing Mojo beers only."

The redhead shrugged. "You're not missing too much. The Horseman is your basic sports bar with a weird old timey theme as an excuse to decorate with dark wood and pretend it's sophisticated."

"Thanks for the warning," Lewis said. "Sounds like a pass for me."

"Do you want some cake?" the redhead asked, nudging two plates, one of each type his way. "I'll let you have some early, so you don't have to wait in line."

"I appreciate that, thank you," Lewis said, relaxing his posture. He set the drinks down on the table and picked up the vanilla cake, taking a bite. "Yum."

"I know, right?" she said, sneaking her own vanilla slice. "Braverton Bakery."

"Do you work there?" Lewis asked.

"Oh, no. I work at the Pinwheel with Layla. Avery's my boss. I'm helping out. I don't have, like, a date or anything. I mean, I came to the wedding with friends, but they're all paired up. I enjoy working, it's good to have things to do." She sucked in a deep breath and stuffed another bite of cake into her mouth.

Lewis allowed what he liked to think of as his *ah, you're not annoying, you're adorably nervous* grin to pull the corners of his mouth up.

"I get it. I enjoy working too. I've been sleeping on the couch in my boss's den for the past few days to be closer to work." And to get away from his insufferable ex who informed him she didn't have money to pay her share of the January rent and he would have to cover her. Again. Somehow twisting things so it seemed like it was all his fault she was so irresponsible.

"Do you live far from Braverton?" the redhead asked.

He nodded and started in on the chocolate cake. "I have an apartment in Troutdale, which made sense when I was working at Edgefield."

"Are you looking to move to the Westside?" she asked and then shook her head. "I'm sorry, we haven't even exchanged names. I'm Beatrix, you can call me Bea."

"Lewis," he said, extending his hand toward her. She gave his palm a firm grip and

shook it. Lewis suspected she had to com-
pensate for being petite the way he did for
being tall. Always adjusting not to appear to
be too much or too little more than what you
were. "Nice to meet you Bea. Although, I
might call you Beatrix. How often do you
meet someone with an X in their name?"

She smiled up at him. "No one's ever said
that to me. I like it. Yes, call me Beatrix."

"And please never call me Lew," he said,
cringing. "It feels like nails on a chalkboard."

"Got it," Bea said. "Hey, so, what I was getting at before was if you were needing a place to
live on the Westside, I need a roommate. You'd
have your own bedroom and bath and you can
have the parking space. I don't have a car. Your
half of the rent will be nine hundred and
ninety-five dollars, water, and trash included."

"You'd let some strange man that you met
at a wedding move in with you?" Lewis asked,
finishing his second piece of cake.

Bea shrugged. "Well, I either need to find
a roommate or another job before January.
Desperate times call for desperate measures."

"I was only kidding," Lewis said. "I
promise I'm not a creep."

Bea screwed up her mouth. "I feel like that's something a creep would say, Lew. Don't be gross."

He scrunched up his shoulders and closed his eyes. "Noooooo, you said it." He put his hands over his ears.

When he opened his eyes, she was smirking up at him. He dropped his hands. "How do I know you're not a creep?" he asked, raising an eyebrow at her.

"You don't," Bea said.

Lewis' laugh boomed. "Okay," he said. "When can I move in? I don't have a ton of things. Just a bed and a dresser and some pots and pans. My current roommate can keep the couch and dining set. She picked them out."

"Uh-oh," Bea said. "You won't be leaving another person high and dry by moving in with me, will you?"

"No," Lewis said, although technically it wasn't true. He'd pay Simone's January rent from his savings and then she'd be on her own. "I should've moved out a long time ago."

"Are you doing anything the day after

Christmas?" Bea asked. "The snow should be melted by then."

"The twenty-sixth would be great," Lewis said, taking his phone out of his pants pocket. "Can I get your phone number and the address?"

Bea took the phone from him and typed the information in.

The DJ brought the music down and everyone turned to look at him. "Ladies and gentlemen, it's time for Ryan and Avery to cut the cake. If you could, please join them at the table on the right side of the atrium."

"I guess that's your cue," Lewis said, clearing the table of his and Bea's cake plates and his two beverages. "We can talk more later."

"Definitely, definitely," Bea said, manning the cake table like she was preparing for battle.

Lewis walked across the room to the drinks station, passing Layla on the way.

"Did I see you got Bea's digits?" Layla asked, a smile in her voice.

"Even better," Lewis said. "Beatrix and I are moving in together."

*B*ea watched Lewis walk back over to the drinks station, stopping to talk to Layla for a second. Whatever he said to her, Layla was headed for Bea with her mouth wide open in shock.

Served her right. Ever since Avery and Layla had gotten their love lives sorted out, they were on a mission to get everyone they knew paired up. Jamie and Meghan were their last victims.

Bea wanted no part of it. Getting into a relationship while in recovery was a bad idea. Getting into a relationship with a brewer while in recovery was an even worse idea.

Bea would have to lay down some rules with Lewis she hoped he would respect. She got the feeling he was a decent guy, and he had a good sense of humor, so she was certain they'd get along just fine.

As roommates.

Layla marched up to Bea and grabbed her by the shoulders. "You're moving in together?" she asked. "I thought maybe he'd ask you to dance or take you out for coffee, not go straight to practically married."

Bea rolled her eyes. "He needs a place to live on the Westside to be closer to work and I need a roommate since I quit the Horseman. We got to talking and figured out a mutually beneficial situation."

"You don't think he'll bring alcohol into the apartment, do you?" Layla asked. "I should've vetted him better."

Bea chuckled. "It's okay. I think he'll be respectful. I already told him I don't drink."

"Yeah," Layla said. "But it might help to explain why."

"I will," Bea said. *Eventually.*

 *B*ea and Lewis stood by the front
door to their apartment staring at
all of Lewis' belongings. As it turned out, Simone did not want to keep the couch or the
dining set, unless she could light them on fire
and propel them at Lewis' head.

"If we angle your couch like this..." Bea
started, grabbing hold of the arm of his navy
blue puffy Ikea monstrosity and turning it so
it was wedged perpendicular to her much
nicer blue and green vintage sofa, "... then we
can group the end tables together to make a
coffee table and put the coffee table next to
the front door underneath the coat hooks

and put our bags or some decorative bowls for keys and gloves on it or something?"

"Decorative bowls are one of the few things I didn't bring," Lewis said, laughing. "I do like the way you're thinking, though. Maybe switch out the TV stand for the coffee table since it's narrower?"

"Yes!" Bea said.

Lewis lifted the TV up while Bea scooted the TV stand out of the way and pushed the coffee table into its space. He set down the TV and carried the stand over to the area by the door.

"All right," Bea said, rubbing her hands together. "Now we just need to figure out how to fit two dining tables and eight chairs in a nook meant for a café table and two chairs."

"Being a wizard would come in so handy right now," Lewis said.

Bea slapped her forehead with her palm. "Duh. If you don't mind, the guys next door could use a kitchen table and chairs. They eat standing at the sink most of the time."

"Yeah, that's completely cool," Lewis said. "Let's give it to someone who'll use it." He started stacking the chairs. "What made you think of that?"

"When you said wizard. Troy and Curt own Old Town Games and Jamie works there and they're always talking about wizards and dragons and that sort of nerdy stuff."

Lewis noted she said nerdy in a matter-of-fact way, no mockery or judgment in her tone.

"I've been dying to hit up their store," Lewis said, not sure if he should admit the middle drawer of his dresser was packed full of Magic cards.

"You should," Bea said. "They have Magic tournaments at least once a month."

"How'd you guess?" Lewis asked.

Bea smirked. "I carried in that dresser drawer."

"Oh, ha," Lewis said. He picked up the stack of four chairs. "If you'll open the door and make the introductions for me, I'll do the heavy lifting."

Bea swung the front door open, winging it into the TV stand with a thud. "I'll remember that's there next time," she said. "Promise."

Lewis followed her out of their apartment onto the landing while she walked into the apartment next door without even knocking.

Three men were sitting in their pajama pants on the carpeted floor of the family room, playing Terraforming Mars on a beat-up coffee table.

"This is Lewis," Bea said as the men greeted her, none of them the least bit irritated by her intrusion. "He's my new roommate. We have an abundance of furniture and I thought maybe you all could use a table and chairs."

One man jumped up. "Awesome," he said. "I wondered what you were doing over there, Bea. I thought you were rearranging again." He clapped Lewis on the shoulder. "I'm Jamie, Bea's best friend. What's up, Lewis? I'll help you bring the table over."

Lewis set the chairs down. He shook Jamie's hand, noting the direct eye contact the man was giving him while doing so. Best friend, huh?

"This is Troy and Curt," Bea said, pointing to the two men on the floor, who each waved when she said his name. She kicked Jamie in the shin until he broke eye contact with Lewis.

"Hi, everyone," Lewis said with a wave.

"Oh, man," Troy said. "We've got Barry White for a neighbor. Nice."

Lewis smiled and turned to Jamie. "Ready to get the table?"

The two men went next door and Bea stayed behind, chatting up Troy and Curt.

As Lewis removed the leaf from the table to make it easier to carry, Jamie put a hand on his shoulder.

"What are your intentions with Bea?" Jamie asked.

Lewis raised his eyebrows. "My intentions?" he said. "I intend to get along with my new roommate, who happens to be a woman. Don't worry, I won't get in the way of whatever *your* intentions with Beatrix are."

Jamie shook his head. "It's not like that. I'm in a relationship," he said, taking the leaf from Lewis and leaning it against the breakfast bar. "Bea has been through a lot and she's a great person. I don't want to see her get hurt."

Lewis nodded. "I get that, man. My last

roommate was my girlfriend for two years and my ex for one. I'm not looking to get into a situation like that again. I just want to live closer to work." The two men hoisted up the table and rotated it onto its side so it would fit through the door. Lewis grinned, thinking about how he and Bea had rolled it in.

"Where do you work?" Jamie asked.

"I'm a craft brewer at Mojo," Lewis said.

Jamie halted and almost dropped his side of the table. "Bea told you she doesn't drink, right?"

"Yes," Lewis said, setting his end of the table down. Apparently, he and Jamie were still having a Bea conversation. "She mentioned it at the wedding when we met."

"Okay," Jamie said, his voice low, "but Bea really, really doesn't drink. You get my meaning?"

Lewis furrowed his brow. "Is it against her religion or something?" he asked.

"I'd rather she be the one to tell you this," Jamie said. "But knowing Bea like I do, she probably doesn't want you to think less of her."

"Why would I think less of her?" Lewis

asked. He knew this situation was too good to be true.

"Bea's in recovery," Jamie said. "She's been sober for two years. You absolutely can't bring your work home with you."

"Oh," Lewis said, considering how often he brought beer home. It wasn't often. "That's cool. It shouldn't be an issue."

"Really?" Jamie asked.

"Really," Lewis said. "I will respect her sobriety."

"Ugh," Bea said from the doorway. "Jamie! Seriously. I was going to tell him."

Jamie's face burned bright red. "Sorry. It just came up."

"It's fine, Beatrix," Lewis said. "Congrats on your two years."

"Thank you," Bea said, grabbing the table leaf and then stepping out of the way. "Will you two bring the table over already? The guys want to set their game up again."

Lewis and Jamie picked the table back up and moved past Bea, Jamie smiling at her apologetically. "I'm sorry I older brothered you," he said.

Bea rolled her eyes. "All is forgiven."

"Older brothered?" Lewis asked, backing into the guys' apartment.

"I have three older brothers," Bea said. "I give off a little sister vibe. Men always feel like they have to protect me." She narrowed her eyes at Jamie. "But they don't."

"Ah," Lewis said. He and Jamie set the table down and adjusted it to the space. "I get it. I'm a little brother."

"Like, figuratively, too?" Bea asked, as Troy and Curt swooped in with their game and took over the table.

"No," Lewis said, laughing. "My brother and I are about the same height."

"You two want to join in on the game?" Curt asked. "We can start over. It's a five player."

"Thanks," Lewis said, "but I've got more furniture rearranging to do. Another time, though. I love Terraforming Mars."

"I'm going to put all of his kitchen stuff away where I like it," Bea said. "I'll check you guys later." She caught Jamie, who was seated at the table, in a headlock and ruffled up his hair. "Enjoy your game."

"Thanks, Bea. Love you," Jamie said.

"Nice to meet you, Lewis. Thanks for the table."

Lewis waved goodbye and followed Bea out of the apartment, shutting the door behind him. "Were you going to tell me?" he asked as they went into their apartment.

"Yes. Of course," Bea said, heading into the kitchen and opening all the cabinets and drawers. "I had an entire speech and a set of rules prepared."

Lewis sat down at the breakfast bar and watched Bea commingle their kitchen supplies. "Lay it on me."

Bea shrugged. "There's no point now. You got the gist. Please don't bring alcohol into our house. Ever. If it's an absolute necessity for work, then you can put it in the guys' fridge, but I can't guarantee it won't get consumed."

"Ah," Lewis said. "So they drink?"

"Just not around me," Bea said, organizing the silicone spatulas by size and rainbow color order.

"It won't be a big deal, I promise," Lewis said. "I'll be at work a lot. You'll hardly ever see me."

"And no parties," Bea said, moving on to

the cutlery drawer. "A few friends are cool, but no ragers, okay?"

Lewis laughed. "You're the closest thing to a non-work friend I have," he said. "How raging things get around here is solely up to you."

Bea giggled. "How old are you?" she asked. "I'm twenty-five going on sixty."

"Twenty-eight. I do feel like I'm old and boring already. Which differs from successful and settled, as my parents like to point out."

"Are they successful and settled?" Bea asked, nesting his and her abundance of mixing bowls.

"No, they're old and boring, but my older brother is the epitome. He's a cardio-thoracic surgery resident at Johns Hopkins, married to an infectious disease researcher. They have two boys and live in a five-bedroom house."

"Okay," Bea drawled. "That is impressive. I hope they enjoy their life as much as you enjoy yours."

Lewis tilted his head, considering her words. "You're right. I do enjoy my life. Especially now that I have a new place to live."

Bea smiled, putting a dusty stockpot in

the sink and washing it with a squirt of dish soap. "Did you always want to brew beer?" she asked.

"No," Lewis said. "I got into it as a hobby while I was in undergrad. Then, when I got a serving job at a brewpub during grad school, I would hang out with the brewers and they'd teach me things. Eventually, that turned into a career in brewing."

"You went to grad school? That's cool," Bea said.

Lewis shrugged. "It was a waste of money. My degree is in organic chemistry and I don't foresee using it beyond what I do now, crafting beers."

"I didn't go to college," Bea said. "I started serving in high school—I'm from Phoenix—and when I moved up here with my boyfriend, Chris, I got the job at the Pinwheel and he worked at a trucking company welding trailers." She shrugged. "I've thought about doing the landscape architecture program at BCC, but that's not happening anytime soon."

"Well," Lewis said, grabbing a dish cloth and taking the pot from her to dry it. "You may feel like you're sixty, but you have a lot of life left to figure out what you want to do."

"Thanks for that," Bea said. She pointed to the cupboard next to the stove. "Put the stockpot on the bottom shelf next to the double-boiler." She quickly washed the lid and handed it to him. "With the lid on."

Lewis did as she asked. It was where he would've put the stockpot, too.

3

"Tell Meghan I say hi," Bea said as she hopped out of Jamie's car.

"Will do," Jamie said. "See you at work tomorrow. Do you have a ride?"

"I'll figure something out. Don't worry," Bea said. She shut the door and began walking upstairs to her apartment.

"Hey, roomie," Lewis said from behind her.

Bea startled and spun around. Even after two weeks of sharing the apartment, Lewis was at work so often she sometimes forgot she didn't live alone. "Hey," she said. "You scared me."

"Sorry," he said, holding a flat cardboard box out to her. "A peace offering."

Bea took the box and smelled it. Ham and green olive. Her favorite. "A pizza offering," she said, continuing up the stairs.

"I was going to say that but then decided to leave the terrible puns to my dad," Lewis said.

Bea stood to the side and waited for Lewis to unlock the door. He motioned for her to go in front of him.

She heard Lewis drop his keys into the decorative bowl she'd put on the table by the door and grinned to herself as she took the pizza into the kitchen.

Bea got two plates down from the cabinet and opened the pizza box, setting two pieces of pizza on each plate. She could've been all dainty and feminine and only put one piece on hers, but she never just ate one piece, so why bother with appearances?

Lewis came around the corner, two bottles of root beer in his hand. He set them on the counter and pulled out one drawer, then another. "Do you know where the bottle opener is?"

Bea reached across the galley kitchen, accidentally brushing her hand against Lewis' arm, and pulled out the one drawer he hadn't looked in. "All seldom-used utensils are in here," she said.

He popped the bottles of root beer open and followed her over to the kitchen table.

Bea paused for a moment, plates of pizza in hand, unsure whether to seat them next to or across from one another.

Lewis chose for her, setting the drinks across from each other. Bea put the plates on the table and took her seat.

"Should I put some music on?" Bea asked, wondering if it was appropriate or if it seemed too date-like. She never put music on when she ate by herself.

"Sure," Lewis said. "Whatever you want. I like some ambiance." He reached for a paper napkin from the holder on the table, shook it out, and tucked it in the collar of his crew-neck sweater.

Bea giggled. She got up, going to the bookshelf containing her record collection, which was jammed next to a small desk behind her couch, and chose an upbeat jazz album. "I think this is just right for the kind of ambiance you inspire."

She put the record on the turntable, soft music spilling from the speakers sitting on either side of the desk.

"It's groo-vy," Lewis said, his voice making the word sound even groovier.

Bea sat down and dug into her pizza.

"I'm glad you're hungry," Lewis said. "I was afraid you'd eaten already."

"No, I'm famished," she said. "Thank you. Usually Jamie and I stop to get a bite after we teach a workshop, but he was eager to get to Meghan's, so we came straight home."

"I know," Lewis said, wiping his mouth with his napkin bib. "I was behind you the entire way home." He finished his first piece of pizza. "It seems silly you and I aren't car-pooling. That way Jamie wouldn't have to bring you home when he has other places to go."

"Actually," Bea said. "I do need a ride to-morrow, if you're offering. Maybe we could set up a schedule and I can chip in on gas like I do with Jamie."

"Great," Lewis said, sipping on his root beer. "This is nice, you know. You are a pleasant human to hang out with."

"Ditto," Bea said, noticing he was almost

done polishing off his second piece. "I'm just going to bring the box to the table."

"Do it," Lewis said. "Let's finish that bad boy off."

Bea stopped. "Okay but save me a piece for breakfast. It's even better in the morning."

"I promise," Lewis said.

Bea grabbed the pizza and put it on the table between them.

"How was your workshop this evening?" he asked. "I believe the sign in the window said it was entitled Calming Calathea?"

"It was great," Bea said. "I hadn't taught this one before, but I am a bit of a Calathea enthusiast."

"I hadn't noticed," Lewis said, deadpan, directing his gaze to the southern facing floor to ceiling shelf of plants blocking entry to their balcony.

"You don't mind, do you?" Bea asked. "I realize it's a bit of a fire hazard, but that area gets the best light in the apartment."

Lewis studied her with his gaze for an instant and then looked away. "I don't mind at all. They're beautiful, Beatrix."

She loved the way her name sounded in

the rich tone of his voice. It sent a thrill of electricity through her.

"What time is work for you tomorrow?" Lewis asked, sliding another piece of pizza from the box onto his plate. "I generally like to be in by nine, but I'm flexible on what time I come home."

"Nine is good," Bea said. "Tomorrow's a short day for me—I work six hours—but I can hang around and wait for you, if that's okay. I can always find something to do."

"All right," Lewis said, polishing off his root beer. "I can be off by five. Maybe we could stop by the grocery store and pick up some things to make dinner? My treat."

Bea tucked her leg underneath her in the chair. "Oh, no you don't. We go fifty-fifty on groceries. And I'll cook since you provided food tonight."

Lewis rubbed his hands together. "Ah, yes! My scheme to get you to cook for me worked."

Bea laughed. "Joke's on you, buddy. I may have a lot of kitchen gear, but that doesn't mean I know how to cook."

Lewis yanked his napkin from his collar

and threw it on the table. "Foiled again!" He leaned toward her. "You're lying, right?"

"Am I?" Bea asked, leaning toward him.

He narrowed his eyes at her, evaluating her poker face, and then gave a sigh of relief. "You are."

"I am," Bea said, giggling. "I'll make chicken enchiladas and a nice salad."

"Why do we, as a people, always say a nice salad?" Lewis asked. "What's so nice about it?"

Bea thought a moment. "Nice as in complementary. I think that's what we, as a people, mean."

Lewis closed the pizza box and carried it into the kitchen, wrapping the last piece in some foil. Bea cleared their plates and bottles.

"This can go in the compost?" Lewis asked, holding up the pizza box.

"It can," Bea said, "but you will have to be in charge if you're going to compost. I'll forget to empty the bin and cause a fruit fly infestation, which is gross and bad for the plants."

"I will take on this responsibility," Lewis said, holding the pizza box to his heart.

"You are so goofy," Bea said, whipping the dish towel he'd left next to the sink at his arm.

Lewis caught hold of it, causing Bea to trip forward, her face smashing into his chest. Her hands shot out, intending to break her fall, but ending up gripping his abs.

Bea froze. She thought she'd left this kind of humiliation behind in her drinking days.

Lewis' abs began to vibrate under her touch, the movement spreading out until his chest was rippling with laughter. Bea didn't know whether to remove her face from him or stay hidden there forever.

He decided for her, wrapping his fingers around her shoulders, and gently pushing her away from him. "You okay?" Lewis asked, the laughter fading and being replaced by concern. "You didn't break your nose or something?"

"No," Bea said, looking down. "I didn't break my nose on your rock-hard abs, Lewis."

He gave a sigh of relief. "But you could've, couldn't you?" He let her go and rubbed his abdomen, shimmying.

Bea cracked a smile that turned into a

giggle fit. "The goofiest," she said, scolding him.

"It's true," Lewis said, turning on the water faucet and squirting some soap onto their plates. "Little known fact, organic chemists are downright zany folk."

Bea picked the discarded dish towel off the floor and held her hand out to accept the washed plate. "Maybe, but have you ever experienced the whimsy of plant people?"

"Whimsy, huh?" Lewis asked.

"Whimsy," Bea said. She put the plates back into the cabinet. "You want to watch some TV?" she asked.

"Can I change into my pajamas first?" Lewis asked.

Bea's heart leapt. "YAS," she said. "The cozier the better."

4

*L*ewis parked his car behind the Mojo building and reached into the backseat to grab his backpack.

"See you at five," Bea said, opening the passenger door, a gust of frigid wind rushing into the car.

"Yep," Lewis said, opening his door and looking up at the heavy, gray sky. "I hope another Arctic Blast isn't coming our way."

"Ugh, me too," Bea said. "Snow makes me almost consider moving back to Phoenix." She shut the door. "Almost."

Lewis waited while she dug around in her gigantic tote bag for her keys to the Pinwheel and made sure she had unlocked the back door before he headed to the back entrance of Mojo.

The Head Brewer, his mentor Arthur, was in the office at his desk doing paperwork and squinting at his computer with his glasses propped on top of his bald head.

Lewis dropped his backpack onto his "desk," which was a two-top high bar table with a wobbly leg, and looked at the brewing schedule Arthur had prepared for him on the clipboard hanging on the wall above it. He took the clipboard from the wall and headed toward the brewery. "Morning, Art," Lewis said on his way out.

"Morning, Lewis," Arthur said, getting his face closer to his computer.

Lewis set the clipboard down on a stainless-steel table and began loading bags of ingredients onto a low cart. He was helping to mix a batch of IPA this morning, so he doubled the hops.

Arthur came into the brewery and waited for Lewis to finish loading the cart. When he'd finished, Lewis pushed it over next to the mash vessel Arthur stood next to. Together, they added the malt to the water, Lewis slashing the bag open and measuring it in a clear, plastic bucket before handing it to Arthur.

Lewis figured he was about another month away from Arthur letting him do this himself. Although he understood why his mentor wanted to be the one to pour the ingredients in—it was his reputation on the line—Lewis felt he'd proven himself.

After they added the ingredients and left the mash to boil, Lewis began cleaning up. Lewis spent a lot of his day cleaning, loading carts, testing beer, and finally tasting it.

Since he'd started living with Bea, he'd been brushing his teeth before going home on the off chance she might smell it on his breath. It was the polite thing to do.

Lewis smiled to himself, thinking about how cute she'd looked in her zebra print fleece pajamas the night before while they were watching TV. She'd curled up on her couch under a hot pink crocheted blanket, while he'd stretched out on his couch wearing his perfectly pedestrian blue and green flannel pajama pants and a ratty OSU t-shirt.

He understood why Jamie older brothered her. Bea appeared fragile because she was short and small-boned, yet she fit Shake-speare's line - *though she be but little, she be fierce.*

Lewis sensed a fire in her, the flames rising, and Bea fighting to contain them for fear she'd lose control. She didn't allow herself to be fully herself. Lewis understood that.

Was it strange he was hoping he would be the person she'd open up to? Why did he want that? Lewis felt his need to keep things platonic between him and Bea slipping. When she'd tripped into him, his first impulse had been to pull her closer into an embrace instead of push her away. He had been goofing around, but he'd also been flirting. Bea probably couldn't tell the difference because he was so awkward.

Yet, he'd caught her looking at him a few times while his eyes were on the TV. Was she considering becoming more than roommates too?

Lewis shook that idea from his mind. Bea wasn't thinking about anyone besides Bea— in a good way. She was focused on bettering her life and didn't need some doofus like him coming along to complicate it.

He should follow her example.

*J*have a problem," Bea said in a whisper to Layla as they were rearranging the begonia table.

"What?" Layla asked. "Is there anything I can do?"

"Well," Bea said. "You caused the problem, so maybe."

Layla narrowed her eyes at Bea. "Is Lewis being a problem? Is he disrespecting you?" She put her hands on her hips. "I don't care how big he is, any bully can be taken down a notch."

Bea grabbed Layla's arms. "He's not a bully. He's a gentle giant. A hot, sweet, funny, gentle giant."

"Oh," Layla said. "So, a problem, but not a *problem*." She smirked. "Do you want to kiss his face? Are you having trouble figuring out how you're going to reach it?"

"Stop," Bea said. "I'm serious. I can't think my roommate is hot and besides, he's totally wrong for me. We're exact opposites."

"I know you've heard the phrase opposites attract, Bea," Layla said. "That cannot be your excuse."

Bea covered her face in her hands. "I need an excuse, though. Otherwise, I will make a bad decision. I'm not going to be able to keep myself from wanting him."

Layla grasped Bea's wrists and lowered her hands from her face. "Honey, you're allowed to want. You're allowed to let people love you. One stupid mistake over two years ago... you gotta be done paying for it at some point. The only person you're hurting then and now is yourself."

"But what if he doesn't want me back?" Bea asked.

"Impossible," Layla said.

Bea crossed her arms. "Not impossible. Chris discovered he didn't want me after I stopped being the party girl he fell in love with."

"Chris is an idiot. He was never right for you and should not be the man you measure all other men against, for crying out loud."

"He's the only boyfriend I've ever had," Bea said. "What if I'm not even capable of being in a relationship while sober?"

Layla squared her shoulders. "You are best friends with a man, Bea. You can be in a healthy relationship. All you have to do is to be friends with Lewis and then, you know, act on your desire to kiss him. Voila! Boyfriend."

Bea nodded. "That doesn't seem too daunting." She grinned. "And I've already figured out how to reach his face."

❦

Snow began falling heavily at three, so Pete closed Mojo's early as everyone had PTSD from being stranded during the Arctic Blast.

"Let's head out early too," Arthur said. "We've done all we need to do for the day. Plus, Janice is so much nicer to me now that you're not occupying our family room couch."

"Roger that," Lewis said. Not to mention his feet hung off the end of their couch by at least a foot. He'd woken up each morning with pins and needles.

Lewis gathered his things and hung the clipboard back on the wall above his table. Walking around the building, past the Tiny Tea Shop and the front of Mojo, he rounded the corner and entered the Pinwheel through the front door.

"Hi, Lewis," Layla said from behind the counter. "You all closing early because of the snow?"

"Yeah," he said. "How about you all?"

"Yep," Layla said. "I'm running the daily reports right now." She nodded toward the room near the back of the shop, a mischievous grin spreading across her lips. "Bea's in the meeting room prepping things for the next few workshops."

"Ah," Lewis said. "Okay, thanks." He strode to the meeting room and knocked on the open door.

Bea looked up from the bin of soil she was mixing, her arms elbow deep in the dirt. "Hey, you," she said, her eyes sparkling. "You're early."

"If you're ready to head out, I can go now," Lewis said, ducking through the doorway.

"Sure," she said. "Think it's safe to run to the grocery store real quick? I don't know that we have much to eat at home." She shook her hands and wiped the dirt from them with a wet cloth, then dried them with a paper towel.

Lewis picked up the lid to the bin leaning against the side of the table and set it on top for her. "As long as we don't need any milk or bread, we should be good."

"Or kale," Bea said, in on the joke. "People in the Portland metro seem to clear the stores of kale when a storm's a'comin'."

Lewis wrinkled his nose. "I never need kale, storm or not."

"Agreed," Bea said. She set the bin on the floor in the corner. "Let me just grab my jacket and bag."

Lewis followed her out into the hall while she put her coat on and opened the door to the parking lot for her.

Bea looked up as she walked outside, snowflakes clinging to her eyelashes. "I think this is going to be pretty snow," she said. "Nothing too dangerous."

Lewis forced himself to look away from her with her face turned up like that, her mouth begging to be kissed. He cleared his throat. "Agreed," he said, echoing her earlier comment.

They got into the car and drove to the

Braverton Market, which was situated halfway between Old Town and their apartment.

The parking lot was busy, so Lewis pulled into a spot along the edge of the road. "Do you mind the walk?" he asked. "It will be easier to get in and out from here than fighting through that mess."

"I'm good," Bea said, nodding down to her feet. "I've got my boots on. Didn't you notice they make me a whole two inches taller?" The corner of her mouth ticked up in a grin.

Lewis nodded. "Oh, I noticed. Miles of difference."

"You did not," she teased, opening her door. "It's okay. It must be hard to see all the way down here from all the way up there."

Lewis got out of the car, falling into step next to Bea. "For real, I can tell now," he said. "The top of your head *is* closer."

She laughed and then slipped on a slick patch of blacktop, grabbing onto his arm to keep from landing flat on her back. "Whoa!"

Lewis bent his forearm up and held it steady while Bea got her feet under her. "You

45

okay?" he asked. "Better hold on to me, those boots have lousy traction."

Bea nodded and wrapped her hand more securely around his biceps. "Thanks."

They made it into the store without further incident. Lewis wished he could come up with a good reason for Bea to continue to hold on to his arm.

"Cart or basket?" she asked.

"Let's get a basket," Lewis said. "I'll carry it and you fill it."

Bea retrieved a basket from the stack and handed it to him. "Produce or enchilada stuff first?" Bea asked.

"Enchilada stuff," Lewis said. "That way we won't smush the produce?"

Bea nodded and weaved through the crowded store to aisle eight, picking up tortillas, a can of enchilada sauce, two cans of black beans, a can of diced tomatoes with chiles, and a bag of rice. Lewis tossed in a couple tall cans of the good coconut water with pulp, not the thin healthy stuff, and then hurried after Bea who was already rounding the corner of the aisle.

He found her in the meat department, debating over which package of chicken breasts to get. She did *not* like to make decisions.

Lewis took the package she was holding in her hands and set it in the basket. "This one's fine."

She peered into the basket. "Ooh, you got the good coconut water. Yum." Bea turned away from him and rushed in the opposite direction toward produce.

Lewis watched as she squeezed between the throngs of shoppers, quicker than he could travel through the store, and people got out of the way for him.

"All nice salads start with a bag of butter lettuce," Bea said when he caught up with her. She dropped one into the basket. "The tomatoes and cucumbers look kind of gross right now. What's your opinion on radishes, red onion and beets?"

"Perfectly nice, nice enough, and weird with enchiladas?" Lewis said.

"You're right," Bea said. "I don't know what I was thinking. Carrots?"

"Nicely nice," Lewis said.

"Ranch or Italian dressing?"

"Chipotle ranch," Lewis said, taking the jar from the cold case by the bagged salads.

"Awesome," Bea said. "Let's get to getting."

"Should we get dessert?" Lewis asked.

"Sure," Bea said. "Nothing big like a whole cake though, I have a horrible sweet tooth and will eat the entire thing."

"Ah, now I know why you gave me two pieces of cake at the wedding," Lewis said. "You wanted to feel less guilty about also wanting two."

Bea stared up at him, her eyes wide. She composed herself. "Maybe," she said, before turning around and hurrying to the bakery section.

They concluded that half a dozen mini chocolate cupcakes was a reasonable dessert for two people, allowing for Lewis to have four instead of three if Bea felt like she was going overboard with more than two.

"It's eerie how well you get me," Bea said as they got into the line, which practically reached all the way to the back of the store.

Lewis shrugged. "Organic chemistry."

Bea rolled her eyes. "You mean I'm like, formulaic?"

"No," Lewis said, keeping his eyes trained on hers. "We've got it."

*ea couldn't be sure she'd never passed out in a grocery store be-fore, but if so, this would be the first time she remembered. Her heartbeat pounded in her ears as she stared up into Lewis' intense gaze.

"Agreed," she said, managing the one word.

He licked his lips. "So, we're on the same page?" he asked.

"Would you two get a move on before someone cuts in front of you?" said a man from behind them, his cart full of milk and bread and toilet paper.

"Sorry," Bea said to the man, wrapping her hand around Lewis' forearm and pulling him forward. "Yes," she said squeezing his arm. "We're on the same page."

When it came time to pay, Lewis stuck his debit card into the card reader before Bea had a chance to get her grocery cash out of her wallet.

"You get it next time," he said.

"Fine," Bea said, not mad about it at all. The scandalous thought occurred to her that if they were on the same page, he could buy her some dinner ingredients. She blushed at the thought while she searched for the re-usable grocery bags she kept in her tote, holding them up triumphantly when she found them. "Ta-da!" she said.

Lewis took one bag from her and loaded it while she loaded the other. They walked out of the store, hand in hand, each holding one bag of groceries. Lewis' bag contained all the cans.

5

ea awoke late the next morning to soft music coming from her turntable in the family room. Avery had called the night before to tell her not to come in today. Another twelve to fourteen inches of snow was predicted, so they'd have to take things day by day, depending on this weird weather.

Lewis had received a similar call from Arthur, who Bea now knew was his mentor, adding that if anyone had to go in, Arthur would be the one to do it.

She showered and got dressed, wanting to look pretty for Lewis even though she knew he'd accept her in her zebra printed pajamas.

Dinner the night before had been great again, both the food and the company. Lewis had made the nice salad while she'd prepared the enchiladas. They'd split the mini cupcakes in half after Bea decided she was in the mood to have three. Lewis washed the dishes while she dried. They'd listened to more jazz and watched more TV, snuggled up together on his couch. And then, when they didn't feel like watching TV any longer, they'd looked out the sliding glass door through the shelf of plants and watched it snow.

It was a magical way to end the evening. When they said goodnight at her bedroom door, Bea had thought Lewis was going to kiss her, but he'd simply squeezed her hand and gone into his room.

She'd been a little disappointed, but then felt silly. They should be, and were, taking things slow.

Bea opened the door to her bedroom and walked down the hall to find Lewis hanging over the arm of her couch, going through her record collection, pulling out one title at a time, marking its place with his finger while he read the jacket, and then putting it back in its space.

After doing this a few times, he noticed Bea watching him from the corner of the room.

"Good morning," he said backing onto the couch and sitting up straight. "Your record collection is on point. I've got a lot of the same albums on my phone, but I think they sound better on vinyl."

"Me too," Bea said, walking over and sitting cross-legged next to him on the couch.

"Do you like to dance?" Lewis asked.

"Do you?" Bea asked, surprised, and excited he might.

He stood, offering her his hand. "I get what you're saying," Lewis said. "How can an oaf like me have any rhythm? The answer is, I don't, but I don't care."

Bea grabbed his hand, unfolding her legs from under her and springing off the couch. "Same!"

Bea let herself go, dancing with her eyes closed like she used to do when she was in the apartment alone. It didn't feel any different. She wasn't embarrassed. Instead, she was having a fantastic time losing herself in the music alongside someone she liked a lot.

When the fast track ended and a slow

one started, Lewis tapped her on the shoulder and nodded to the side tables turned coffee table. "Hop up."

Bea stepped onto one of the tables, finding that it put her almost at eye level with Lewis.

He wrapped his arms around her waist, and she slung hers around his neck, their faces inches apart. "I should've kissed you last night," Lewis said, his eyes staring at her mouth. "I don't know how fast you want to take this." He brought his eyes up so that his gaze met hers. "You take the lead."

Bea closed the distance between their mouths, pressing her lips to his, the whiskers from his beard tickling her chin.

He flattened his hands against her back, urging her closer still.

"How long have you been thinking about doing this?" Bea asked, her lips brushing over his.

"The wedding," Lewis said. "Every day since, even though I almost convinced myself I didn't want to a couple of times."

"I've been lying to myself, too," Bea said. "I don't want to be scared anymore, Lewis.

You make me feel safe and cared for. Things I never thought I'd feel again."

Lewis hugged Bea to him. "I feel safe with you and can trust you're not playing games with me."

Bea nuzzled her face into Lewis' neck, and they stayed that way, rocking back and forth to the music until the A side of the record ended.

"Hey," Lewis said, drawing his head back, so they were face-to-face again. "The Mojo employee holiday party is next Monday night. Would you be able to go with me?"

"Our first public appearance as roommates who are more than roommates?" Bea asked. It suddenly occurred to her she would have to tell Jamie about her and Lewis, and Jamie would have an opinion about it. For once, she wasn't certain what that opinion would be.

"I anticipate kissing you in public prior to Monday night," Lewis said. "But I suppose it will be our first larger event as a couple."

"A couple?" Bea asked, her fingers playing with the hair at the nape of his neck. "Are you asking me to be your girlfriend?"

Lewis nodded. "It feels right."

Bea kissed him again. "It does."

٭

*A*fter another snow day spent at home with Lewis, the two of them dancing and lounging and watching TV and generally being couple-ish, Bea was eager to go into the Pinwheel and reveal her new girlfriend status to her co-workers.

Jamie had been snowed in with his pregnant girlfriend Meghan, and Bea and Jamie hadn't even texted one another the past few days. As her best friend, Jamie's opinion about Lewis mattered the most. Avery and Layla were in a loving love mood right now, so they would be ecstatic, but Jamie would be real with her. He'd let her know if she was making the right decision.

Lewis parked the car and before they got out, he reached over and put his hand on her knee. "Can I kiss you goodbye for the day?" he asked.

Bea leaned toward him, cupping his face in her hands, and let Lewis kiss her. "I'll see you after work," Bea said.

"I'll bring home pizza again," Lewis said.

"Work is going to be wild playing catch-up today. Probably for you, too. We'll be too tired to cook."

"Agreed," Bea said, opening her car door.

They stood in front of Lewis' car, reluctant to leave one another.

"One more kiss," Bea said, going up onto tip toe.

Lewis bent down and kissed her sweetly.

"What is up, neighbors?" Jamie said from behind Bea.

She and Lewis broke off the kiss. Bea turned around to face him.

"Hi," she said, sounding a bit like a kid being caught sneaking in past curfew.

"Hey, Jamie," Lewis said, his voice more confident than hers. "Enjoy the snow days?"

Jamie's eyebrows raised. "It looks like you two did." He fixed his gaze on Bea. "Are congratulations in order?"

"We're together, if that's what you mean," Lewis said, putting his hands on Bea's shoulders.

"Okay, cool," Jamie said, nodding his head and not sounding like he was cool with it at all. He pointed toward the back door of the Pinwheel. "See you inside, Bea."

Bea patted Lewis on the hand and stepped away from him. "Jamie, I'll walk in with you now." She turned and smiled at Lewis. "Have a good day."

"You too, Beatrix," he said.

Jamie waited by the back door, holding it open for Bea.

She hurried to it, not wanting to let all the heat out.

"Who kissed who first?" Jamie asked as they went into the shop.

"I did," Bea said, hanging up her coat and tote bag on a hook. "Lewis left the decision up to me."

"He did, huh?" Jamie said. "Lewis got you to make a decision?"

Bea stuck her tongue out at him. "Shut it."

"You genuinely like him?" Jamie asked. "It's not just convenient and you're feeling left out because everyone else is pairing off?"

"That's hurtful," Bea said, putting her hands on her hips. "I'm allowed to fall in love."

Jamie took off his winter coat and hung it up. "I'm not meaning to hurt you, Bea. This is a big step for someone in recovery, one that Lewis specifically assured me would not happen. But I understand how things can go sideways and before you know it, you're in love. Believe me, I do."

Bea crossed her arms. "Have you told Meghan you love her?" she asked, unable to keep from smiling.

Jamie nodded. "I did. Last night."

"And she said it back?"

Jamie nodded again.

Bea attacked Jamie in a hug. "I'm so happy for you!"

Jamie held her tight. "I want to be happy for you, too. Just please let me know if you need help, okay?" He released her from the hug and held her away from him. "I'll always be here for you, no matter what."

"Same," Bea said, pinching Jamie's cheek. "You are legit going to be a step-daddy," she sang.

"I know," he said.

Layla and Avery stuck their heads out of the door of the meeting room, both with tears in their eyes.

"Congratulations, to you both," Layla said.

"No need to thank us," Avery said. "The

two best matchmakers in Old Town." She and Layla high-fived.

Bea rolled her eyes and took Jamie by the wrist. "C'mon, we better move before their egos burst and get pride all over us."

"You're just happy 'cause you're happy," Layla trilled as she and Avery went back into the meeting room.

❧

*L*ewis sat on Bea's couch waiting for her to finish getting ready for the Mojo employee holiday party. He wasn't dressed much different than usual apart from wearing nicer shoes. At work he wore rubber non-slip black boots so he didn't wipe out on the floor of the brewery. He felt as though putting on brown leather oxfords and wearing a button-up underneath his gray crewneck sweater transformed him into Employee Holiday Party Man.

Bea, on the other hand, had several options in her closet, which led to her having to make several decisions, which led to her having a fashion crisis, which led to a phone

60

call with her manager Layla for some reason, before it was all sorted out.

Lewis thought this was a man not understanding women moment more than a Lewis not understanding Bea moment, though. He'd had a similar brouhaha with Simone before going to an event.

Bea walked out into the family room and did a twirl for him. "What do you think?" she asked.

Lewis drank her in with his eyes. "You're gorgeous. That green dress is beautiful on you." He smiled. "I like your hair up, too. And the shoes are outrageous."

Bea giggled. "I'll just have to hold on to your arm all evening," she said, kicking her foot up, showing off her four-inch black heels.

Lewis stood and approached her, wrapping an arm around her waist, and pulling her to him. "Would you look at that?" he said. "I don't have to get a crick in my neck to kiss you standing up."

"Me either," Bea said, tilting her face up to meet his. "Don't mess up my lipstick... too much," she said.

As their lips met, Lewis still couldn't believe he got to kiss such a wonderful woman, and that she wanted to kiss him back.

What they'd thought would be a major issue between them had turned out to be nothing to worry about. He supposed the real test would be this party where the beer would be flowing, but he had a personal policy of not having more than one drink at work functions anyway, so it wouldn't be a problem.

"Full transparency," Lewis said. "Since I am one of two brewers at Mojo, they will expect me to drink the beer I make."

Bea screwed up her mouth. "Okay," she drawled.

"I'll have a single beer and sip on it throughout the evening. I don't like to overindulge in general and especially not at work."

She nodded. "That seems reasonable." Bea took a deep breath. "I know it's only one beer and you're a big guy and one beer won't make you drunk or anything, but could I please drive us home? I'd feel better if the person behind the wheel was one hundred percent sober."

Bea had yet to drive his car, but he knew

she'd driven Jamie's from time-to-time and Jamie had been fine with it. "Of course," Lewis said. "In fact, why don't you drive us there as well?" He walked over to the decorative bowl he'd gotten in the habit of dropping his keys in and took them out, offering them to her.

"Yeah?" Bea asked. "Cool. I'm a good driver, I promise. Like a granny."

Lewis put on his coat and handed Bea's to her. "That isn't a confidence inspiring comparison," he said, chuckling. "My granny lost her license after she drove into her neighbor's rhododendron." Lewis furrowed his brow. "Come to think of it, my grandpa's truck ended up in a ditch more than once when I was a kid. It might be that my grandparents are terrible drivers."

Bea laughed, dropping Lewis' car keys into a small black leather purse, much smaller than her usual behemoth of a tote bag. "I will strive to not be like them, then."

6

They arrived at the party without incident and Bea was thankful. She'd been in her fair share of fender benders, mostly while sober, but didn't want Lewis to refuse to let her drive his car. She parked in the same spot Lewis always parked in.

"Definitely safer than Granny and Grandpa," Lewis said, opening his door.

Bea checked three times to make sure she'd put the keys into her clutch before getting out and locking the car. Lewis walked around to her side and offered his hand, which she grasped tightly as they made their way to the back door of Mojo.

Bea could feel the vibration of the music bumping in the dining room all the way back by the office. Lewis unlocked the door to the cramped space, helped her out of her coat and set both hers and his onto a bar table in the corner.

"This joint could use some plants," Bea said.

Lewis laughed, nodding. "What? You aren't enjoying the three dudes crammed into a storage closet vibe we've got going?"

"Nope," Bea said. "I'll see if Avery will let me donate a few snake plants to the cause. Those things thrive on neglect."

"Perfect," Lewis said. "I'm sure we'll excel at neglecting them." He kissed the top of her head. "Ready to make our debut?"

"You don't think they all know?" Bea asked. "At the Pinwheel we're so up in each other's business I sort of forget that all co-workers don't act that way."

"I'm sure some of the servers and bartenders know," Lewis said. "In my experience, they're the ones to go to for the hot workplace gossip."

Bea giggled and took his hand. "I'm just picturing the type of hot gossip our evenings in watching Golden Girls reruns must generate."

"Scandalous!" Lewis said, pulling Bea toward the music.

When they entered the room, a few people turned to look at them, but they simply welcomed them to the party and returned to what they were doing.

A small group was dancing in the space where tables usually were. Everyone else was sitting at the booths along the windows, drinking beer and eating pizza, or standing at bar tables, drinking beer and eating pizza.

Lewis led Bea over to the bar. Pete, the owner of Mojo, was plating up squares of their famous Detroit-style pizza, while the man next to him poured drinks.

"Lewis," the drinks guy said. "Glad you made it."

"Bea!" Pete said. "You're here with Lewis?"

Bea and Lewis looked at each other.

"Oh, yeah, they're here together," the drinks guy said. "Get a load of the moony eyes." He extended his hand to Bea. "I'm Art, Lewis' mentor."

Bea shook his hand. "Nice to meet you. I

remember you dancing with your wife at my boss Avery's wedding."

Pete slapped Arthur on the arm with the back of his hand. "This is Bea from next door, you dummy. You've probably seen her a million times in the parking lot."

Arthur held up his hands in defense. "I only have eyes for my Janice. Although, now that you mention it, I don't know how I could miss that pretty red hair."

"Ham and green olive square?" Pete asked, sliding one Bea's way.

"Thank you," Bea said. "My favorite."

"Same for me, please," Lewis said.

"And what can I get for you?" Arthur asked. "Want to start with the IPA and work your way to the stout?" Arthur pushed two pint glasses onto the glass rinser.

"I'll have an IPA," Lewis said. "Bea's going to stick to root beer. She's driving."

"Good, good," Arthur said, pouring their drinks. "Always nice when one half of a couple doesn't mind being the DD."

Bea searched the foggy memories of her time with Chris. Neither of them had ever been the designated driver. She was lucky she wasn't dead or that she hadn't killed someone else.

Never. Again. With each passing day it got a tiny bit easier to be happy about never again putting herself in that situation.

Lewis carried both their drinks in one hand and his plate in the other, choosing a booth next to where people were dancing.

Bea waved at two of the servers she recognized, Holly and Nina, who used to come into the Headless Horseman on Tuesdays for Industry Night.

"Hey, Bea. Hey, Lewis," Holly said, sliding into the booth next to Bea, leaving Nina on the dance floor having a dance battle with two underage busboys.

Bea could tell Holly had had a few, but she'd never seen her be anything but chill and fun when she was drinking.

"Hey," Bea and Lewis said at the same time.

Holly pointed at Bea. "Does Avery still do that radio show on Sunday mornings?"

"Uh-huh," Bea said. "Plantiful Advice. It's on OPB."

"Yeah," Holly said. "I have an aloe that looks like it's about to bite it. I've been meaning to call in, but nine on a Sunday is early, fam, you know?"

Bea giggled. "I do know. Why don't you tell me what's going on with the plant? I'm nowhere near as knowledgeable as Avery, but I know a thing or two."

Lewis chewed his pizza, watching the interaction between Bea and Holly with a grin on his face.

"So, like, it's all shriveled and brown on the ends and then sort of flat and then all fine and plump at the bottom."

"Yay!" Bea said. "I know the answer to this one. So, you need to water your aloe more often."

"Really?" Holly asked. "I've been holding off for, like, a month because I thought I was over-watering it."

"You may have been," Bea said. "It's easy to go to extremes with plants like aloes because they look like trash if you either over or under water them. Some plants, it's so easy to tell, their leaves droop, you give them a good soak, they perk up."

"Totally," Holly said, leaning her elbows on the table.

"I'm going to grab another square," Lewis said. "Bea, Holly, can I bring you anything?"

"I'm good," Bea said.

"Grab me a square and a water, will ya, big guy?"

Bea was happy to hear Holly was going to eat and hydrate.

"Will do, smallish lady," Lewis said, giving Bea a wink.

"So," Bea continued. "What you're going to want to do is stick your finger in the soil to about here..." she pointed to the knuckle of her index finger, "... and if it's dry, then give it a soak. Meaning run it under the tap until water comes out the drainage hole in your pot."

"Drainage hole?" Holly asked. "Huh."

❧

*L*ewis got in the line for food behind two of the bartenders.

"Dude," the brunette man said. "Is she the one who got in a fight with that old lush, Patty, over at Ringler's, and broke her wrist?"

"I do think that's her," the blond man

said. "Total party girl. She and her boyfriend used to come into Bombs Away at, like, three in the afternoon and stay till close."

"Guess she's got a new man now. Easier access," the brunette man joked.

"Right?" the blond man said. "Even though he's twice her size, they've probably got the same tolerance."

Lewis cleared his throat. He'd hoped they weren't talking about Bea, but who else was here with someone twice her size? "My girlfriend's name is Beatrix, and she's sober now," he said when the two men turned around and looked up at him. "I'd appreciate it if you'd quit maligning her."

"Whoa, dude, sorry," the blond man said. "We didn't know you were behind us."

"I gathered that," Lewis said, pointing forward for them to move up in line.

"That's really cool she doesn't drink anymore," the brunette man said. "Good for her because she was a *disaster* back in the day." The blond man elbowed his friend.

"That was then," Lewis said. "This is now."

"Totally," the blond man said, facing away

from Lewis, looking straight ahead, not talking to his friend anymore.

Lewis returned to the table with the squares of pizza and the water for Holly, which she promptly chugged.

"Dancing makes me so thirsty," she said and dug into her pizza with gusto.

Bea excused herself to go to the restroom and Holly let her out of their side of the booth.

"So, how do you know Bea?" Lewis asked, wondering if his new girlfriend was more infamous in Braverton than he'd suspected.

"From the Horseman," Holly said. "She was a server there for a while."

Lewis nodded. "So, not from her drinking days."

Holly shook her head. "Nah, although I've heard things. But it's whatever." She took a bite of her pizza.

"What things?" Lewis asked.

"Do you really want to know?" Holly asked. "It's not who she is now."

"You're right," Lewis said. Hadn't he almost said the same thing to the bartender dudes? "I don't need to know."

Bea returned, reaching around Holly to

retrieve her root beer. She drained her drink and then set it on the table, grabbing Lewis by the arm. "Let's dance!"

Holly finished her last bite of pizza. "I'm here for it."

The three of them joined the others on the dance floor and soon more employees followed. Lewis watched Bea put her hands in the air and bump hips with Holly, both of them laughing.

Bea was in her element. Lewis imagined this used to be what her life was like every night as the resident party girl of Braverton. Now she spent her evenings at home watching TV and staring out the sliding glass door at the weather.

Was that really enough for her?

Was he enough for her?

At first Simone had found him funny and smart but as their relationship progressed and he worked more, she'd lost interest in him. He became a boring, nerdy mansplainer in her eyes, and a lot less funny.

What if the same thing happened with Bea?

She danced her way toward him, attempting to hip bump him, but hitting him squarely in the side of the thigh.

"Not our move," she said, giggling.

Lewis took her hand and spun her out and then reeled her in. "Better?" he asked, lowering his mouth to her ear.

She threw her head back, laughing, and kissed him on the cheek. "The best."

§

They left the holiday party at a respectable hour since they both had to be at work at nine the next day. The servers and bartenders didn't start their shifts until eleven, so their revelry could go on longer.

"That," Bea said as they walked to Lewis' car, "was fun." She found the keys in her purse on the first try and pushed the button on the fob to unlock the doors. "Kind of like my old days, but I won't have a hangover tomorrow and I'll remember everything that happened."

"You don't miss the old days?" Lewis asked, opening the passenger door. He felt silly not driving the car as he was stone cold sober.

Bea shrugged. "Sure, sometimes I do." They got into the car. "What I'm learning, though," she continued, "is that I can still have fun."

As Bea started the ignition, the sky opened and poured rain. "Ack," she said, feeling around the steering wheel. "Where are the windshield wipers?"

"Why don't you let me drive?" Lewis asked. "I'm completely fine and driving an unfamiliar car in the dark and rain has got to be just as impairing as a two-hundred-and-fifteen-pound man having a single pint of beer."

Bea stopped looking for the windshield wipers. He was not Chris, drunk out of his mind, arguing with her. Lewis was being reasonable. Still, Bea felt like she was breaking a promise to herself. Her enjoyment of the evening was becoming a bit tarnished.

"Yeah, okay," she said. "You come around and I'll climb over."

Lewis got out of the car and Bea scooted to the passenger seat. She reached underneath it, adjusting it way forward so she was sitting next to Lewis up front and not in the backseat.

They were both quiet on the way home, but he held her hand as they ran through the parking lot and up the stairwell to their apartment.

"I'm going to change into my pajamas," Bea said, taking off her coat. "Want to watch some TV before bed?"

"Actually," Lewis said, dropping the car keys in the decorative bowl. "If you don't mind, I think I'll hit the hay. Social gatherings exhaust me."

"Oh, sure," Bea said. "I get that." She shrugged. "I'll just go to bed too."

He walked her to her bedroom door and gave her a quick kiss goodnight. Even though it was only one beer and he'd had it a few hours ago, Bea could still smell it on his breath. She was grateful the kiss had been short and sweet.

"Goodnight," Bea said.

"Goodnight," Lewis said, already closing his bedroom door.

7

The next morning, whatever weirdness had gone on between them the night before had seemed to vanish.

As Lewis pulled into the parking spot his car had left twelve hours before, Bea reminded him that she was teaching a workshop that evening.

"I texted Jamie," she said, "and he can bring me home if you don't want to wait or need to stay later."

"I don't mind waiting," Lewis said. "We've been crafting an Imperial stout and if Arthur deems it ready today, I'll need to stay later, anyway."

"Cool," Bea said, smiling. "Just knock on

the back door whenever you get done and I'll let you in."

Lewis leaned over and kissed her thoroughly. "Have a good Tuesday, Beatrix," he said, giving her an extra peck on the forehead.

"I will," she said. "I already can't wait to see you tonight."

Lewis lowered his eyes, smiling. "I feel the same way."

They got out of the car and Lewis kissed her again before officially saying goodbye for the day.

Bea went into the shop, unable to keep the smile off her face. She was navigating an actual grown-up, romantic relationship while sober, and it was working.

Avery came downstairs from her office, which used to be her apartment, with her ever-present cup of tea in her hand. "Good morning, Bea," she said. "How was the shindig at Mojo's?" she asked. "I ran into Pete in the parking lot this morning and he said they didn't shut things down until after midnight."

"Lewis and I left at nine," Bea said, tying on the apron Layla had made her for Christmas. "But it was really fun. Nothing structured, just hanging out and eating and dancing."

"And plenty of drinking? The way Pete was dragging screamed hangover." Avery cringed.

"People were having fun," Bea said. "It's fine."

Avery put the cash box underneath the counter. "I'm covering for Layla today. She got a last-minute appointment to tour a long-term care facility for her mom out in North Plains, so she took the day off."

"Ooh," Bea said, picking up a spray bottle and heading to the shelf of ferns. "I hope she can get her in to this one, although North Plains is a longer drive."

"I think Bradley's nurse, Lachlan, has some connections with this place. She sounded like it was a sure thing."

Bea spent the morning doing her Tuesday chores and helping customers while Avery split her time doing admin stuff in her office and down in the shop checking on Bea.

"I'm so glad Layla gave you more hours," Avery said. "If Jamie leaves us to go work with Meghan, which I'm expecting him to tell me he's going to do any day now, I think we can move you to full time and not have to hire another salesperson."

"Has Jamie said something to you about leaving?" Bea asked. She was grateful that Avery wanted her to be full time, but sad that Jamie hadn't told her first he might leave.

"No, no," Avery said. "It's all speculation on my part, but you know he's drastically lowered his hours at OTG and has been spending all his extra time at the greenhouse. When the baby comes, Meghan's going to be relying on him more than ever."

Bea bit the inside of her lip. She hadn't known that Jamie had cut his hours at OTG. They hadn't had a real talk in a while. "I guess you're right," Bea said. "It won't be the same here without him."

Avery put her arm around Bea's shoulders. "A lot is changing right now, that's for sure, but it's not all bad," she said, lowering her voice. "For instance, Graceann is going to be a big sister before the end of this year."

"What?" Bea asked, turning toward Avery and throwing her arms around her. "Congratulations! Oh, my gosh. How did Ryan take the news? Was he so surprised?"

Avery laughed. "First, he was shocked into silence, then he cried, then he and Graceann danced around the family room like a couple of buffoons. It was pretty much the greatest."

"That is so fantastic," Bea said, her worries about Jamie becoming less about him leaving her and more about her being a better friend and knowing what was going on with him. People moving on with their lives was not a bad thing.

Jamie arrived for his shift shortly after noon. "Hello, planty people," he shouted from the back hall.

"Hello," Bea called back. "Get out here, I need to talk to your face."

He walked to her and braced his hands on her shoulders. "My face is reporting for duty."

"You lowered your hours at OTG?" Bea asked, getting right to it.

"Yeah," Jamie said, lowering his hands. "I didn't tell you? That was dumb of me. I'm helping with monthly inventory and the occasional event. Troy and Curt have it all handled without me, anyway."

"So, does that mean you will cut your

hours here, too?" she asked, rearranging the greeting cards on the checkout counter.

"That I'm not sure of yet," he said. "I'm taking over more and more responsibilities at the greenhouse. Meghan's getting serious about adding me to the payroll. This might be the move for me. Managing Daylight Greenhouse could be my career."

Bea nodded. "I think it's your move too," she said. "We can't stay the same forever, working at the plant shop and living next door to one another."

Jamie pulled her into a hug. "I'm glad you feel that way," he said, "because after February, we won't be neighbors anymore."

She squeezed him as hard as she could, considering merging from hug to head lock. "Dang it, Jamie."

"Do I want to know what's going on here?" Avery said, coming into the room from upstairs. "Bea, it appears you're giving Jamie the Heimlich but from the front, which, FYI is not the proper technique."

"He's moving in with Meghan," Bea said.

"Oh," Avery said. "This scenario makes a lot more sense now. Carry on." She walked back to the storage room.

Jamie raised his hand. "Do I get a say in this?"

"Am I actually hurting you?" Bea asked.

"No, not at all," Jamie said, chuckling. "I appreciate that you love me so much you would try, though." He took hold of her arms behind his back and unclasped them.

She stepped away from him. "Will you watch the front while I go get ready for the workshop tonight? There's a ton to do."

"No problem," Jamie said. "Hey, tonight after, why don't we go grab a bite?"

"Lewis is taking me home," Bea said. "We could all go out together?"

"Cool," Jamie said. "I should get to know him better."

"Well, why don't you invite Meghan too?" Bea said. "A double date."

"Awesome," Jamie said. "See, Bea, this is how you and I stay best friends. Compromise, not violent squeezy hugs."

"I feel like there's a place for both," Bea said, heading to the meeting room.

*L*ewis set the two growlers of Imperial stout on the floor in the back seat of his car. Arthur had gifted them to him, and Lewis didn't want to turn them down. They'd brewed an excellent albeit strong batch.

He imagined the guys next door would enjoy sharing a glass with him. He didn't know about storing it all in their fridge, though. Two growlers took up a lot of room.

Perhaps Bea would let her rule slide this one time? Wasn't a sizeable amount of stout once better than a smaller portion frequently? Lewis was annoyed he had to consider such things, but no relationship was without its compromises. He just had to make sure he wasn't the only one doing the compromising.

He went to the back door of the Pinwheel and knocked twice. Jamie answered the door, holding it open for him.

"Hey, Bea's ringing up the last workshop attendee and then she'll be done. I'm finishing cleaning up. Come on in." Jamie went into the meeting room and Lewis followed.

"Bea and I were talking," Jamie said, sweeping the floor, "about you, me, her and

Meghan all going to grab a bite this evening if that's cool with you."

"Sure," Lewis said, thinking the stout would be fine chilling in the car for a couple hours. "Where do you all want to go?"

Jamie stooped over and swept potting soil into a dustpan. "DeConti's has a good happy hour that starts at nine. I guess we'd usually go to Mojo's or Small's but since it's a double date, we thought we'd be fancy." He stood, dumping the dirt into a metal compost bin before replacing the lid.

"The ladies are good with a happy hour?" Lewis asked.

"Yeah, as long as we're there for discount food and not drinks. It's easier on Bea if everyone she's with isn't drinking. That okay with you?"

"Of course," Lewis said. "The two of us haven't been out enough together for me to know what her triggers are."

"Honestly, at this point I think Bea's only triggers are people driving after drinking and having alcohol in her house. Otherwise, she can handle it." He set the broom in the corner and waved at Lewis to follow him.

"You're welcome to have a beer at my place anytime."

"Yes," Lewis said, sliding past Jamie into the hall. "Bea mentioned that. My only issue is that I have two growlers of Imperial stout sitting in the car right now and I don't know where to store them."

"I don't suppose you can leave them in your car?" Jamie asked, turning off the light in the meeting room.

"Not after they're open," Lewis said.

"Hmm," Jamie said. "We probably don't have enough room in our fridge for two. We could keep one in the fridge and one on our balcony?"

Lewis nodded. "That'll work, thanks." It was a more complicated plan than he would've liked, but at least he would keep his girlfriend happy.

§

Bea walked the last customer out and locked the door behind them, making sure the open sign was turned to closed. Jamie forgot to do that all the time and Bea was forever following up.

"Am I good to turn off the lights?" Bea called to Jamie.

"Yep," Jamie called back. "Lewis is here."

Bea flipped off the lights and headed to the back hall. "My two favorite man people," she said, going up on tiptoe to give Lewis a kiss.

"Hello," Lewis said, smiling down at Bea. "I hear we're going on a double date to De-Conti's?"

"Is that okay?" Bea asked. "I know I should've checked with you first."

Lewis shrugged. "We had zero plans and I'm starving. It's all good."

"Let's head out," Jamie said, putting on his coat.

Lewis handed Bea her coat and held onto her tote while she put her coat on.

Jamie checked his phone. "Meghan's already there. She's going to order a bunch of appetizers and waters. I'm assuming for everyone, but you never know with her. The pregnancy cravings are strong with my lady."

The three of them left the Pinwheel and went to their cars.

Bea smelled the beer as soon as she opened the door. She peered into the backseat and saw two growlers on the floor. "Bringing your work home?" she asked, hoping Lewis wouldn't hear the edge in her voice. Bea wanted so much not to be "that girl" in recovery, but she was. She prepared to go over her rules with Lewis again.

"Sort of," Lewis said. "Arthur gifted those to me. I will keep one in the guys' fridge and one on their balcony. Jamie and I already worked it out."

"Excellent," Bea said, getting into the car, grateful this wasn't going to be a thing. "Thanks."

"It's fine," Lewis said in a tone which told Bea it was not totally fine. "In the future maybe we could keep it in our house, but I won't drink it when you're around? It seems like we're over-complicating this and there's some room to compromise. But maybe I'm being obtuse?"

Bea closed the door but didn't put her seatbelt on. Apparently, this was going to be a thing. "I already compromised last night when I let you drive even though I didn't want you to," Bea said. "It's your turn to compromise. Storing the beer over at the guys' house isn't that complicated. I don't get why you think it is." She crossed her arms.

Lewis put the keys in the ignition but didn't start the car. "It's complicated because it's my beer, from my work, my *career*, that I should be able to have in the apartment I pay half the rent on," he said. "I shouldn't have to go over to the neighbor's apartment and bother them. I should be able to keep it at mine and partake of it whenever I want. I mean, the product of your work is blocking the way to our balcony and I'm supposed to be okay with that?"

Bea rolled her eyes. "You're not tempted to eat the houseplants and if you had a problem with them blocking the door, you could've said something to me and we could've figured it out." She shook her head. "This fight is stupid. You're being stupid."

"Am I?" Lewis said, his voice gruff. "Because I think you're being childish. You've been sober for two years, Bea. Time to get over it."

"I'm an alcoholic, there's no getting over it," Bea said, throwing open the door and jumping out of the car. She slammed the door closed and began walking toward De-Conti's. Jamie would give her a ride home.

Bea heard Lewis start the car and then he pulled up beside her, the window rolled down.

"Get in the car, Beatrix. I'm not done talking about this with you."

She stopped walking, but kept her head forward, not looking at him. This morning she couldn't wait to see him again, and now she couldn't stand the sight of him. "Can you please just go home? I don't want to be around you right now."

After a moment, Lewis sighed heavily and then spoke. "Fine. I'll go home. Will you get a ride with Jamie?"

Bea nodded, pulling her coat tighter around her body.

"You feel safe to walk there this time of night?" Lewis asked.

"Just go," Bea said, her rage bubbling up. She started walking again. If he knew what was good for him, he'd listen before they both said more things they'd regret.

"Suit yourself," Lewis said. He rolled up the window and drove past her, taking a right onto Main Street, heading home.

*L*ewis banged the heel of his hand on the steering wheel. What had just happened? Why had he been so stubborn and forced the issue? Bea was right, she'd compromised last night, at least to her that had seemed like a compromise.

Still, he hated it when people walked away from an argument. Simone had never done that. Quite the opposite, she'd worn him down until he fell silent and gave in to whatever she wanted.

He'd thought Bea was the one with all the baggage, but Lewis had to face facts. He had his fair share of triggers and baggage too.

Lewis turned the radio up, hoping to drown out his own thoughts. By the time he was parking in his space at the apartment, he'd chilled out some. He grabbed the growlers from the backseat of the car and carried them upstairs, knocking on the guys' door with his knee.

Troy answered. "Hey, man, what's up?" he said, eyeing the growlers. "Is that the Imperial stout? Jamie texted to say you'd be dropping it by sometime tonight for safe keeping."

Lewis handed the stout to Troy. "You can have it."

"Really?" Troy asked, hefting the growlers one in each hand. "Do you want to come in and have a glass?"

Lewis hesitated. Yes, he wanted to come in for a glass. No, he did not want to further anger his girlfriend by smelling like beer when she got home. "I shouldn't. Bea and I had a fight over it, and she's gone out on our double date with Meghan and Jamie alone."

"Ah-ha," Troy said. "Well, I could have Jamie text me when they're on their way home. That way, you can come in for a quick glass, brush your teeth, and get home with Bea none-the-wiser. It's up to you, but I think you deserve to drink the fruits of your labor."

"Oh, all right," Lewis said, stepping into the apartment. He felt a tiny bit deceitful, but he was technically following Bea's rules.

*L*ewis awoke to the sound of the alarm on his phone blaring from his pants pocket. He was sleeping on a couch, his legs hanging over the arm. It was not his couch. Even without opening his eyes, he knew he was not on his own couch in his own apartment.

He stuck his hand into his pocket and silenced the phone. Then, and only then, did he open his eyes. His head was pounding and the morning light streaming in from the guys' balcony doors seemed to be aimed at his face.

Lewis sat up too quickly, a wave of nausea charging through him. He took a deep breath and looked around the room, trying to remember how he'd ended up sleeping here and not in his own apartment on the other side of the wall.

That's when he saw the growlers and three empty pint glasses sitting on the breakfast bar. Images of the night before flashed through his head.

He'd had more than one quick glass of stout. Troy had poured the first, but he'd poured the second, third, fourth, and fifth.

Imperial stout was strong stuff. The limit at Mojo's was one. No wonder he felt like dying.

Terraforming Mars was laid out on the dining table, a few pieces scattered on the floor. They'd started a game, but Curt had tapped out to go to bed. Lewis recalled laughing as Curt stumbled down the hall, running into the wall and knocking a framed poster down.

Jamie had texted Troy, but Troy forgot to check his phone.

Bea had come into the apartment, fuming, saying that even next door was too close for her when she could hear them carrying on from the parking lot. She'd poured the rest of the beer into the kitchen sink, told Lewis it was over between them, and gone to stay with Jamie at Meghan's.

Troy shuffled out into the hallway from his bedroom, rubbing his temples with his fingertips. "So many regrets," he said.

Lewis nodded, the pressure of moving his head up and down felt like his brain was bashing against his skull.

"Hey, man," Troy said. "I will grovel with Bea on your behalf. Last night was one hundred percent my doing. Never should've convinced you to hang out."

"Nah," Lewis said. "I'm a big boy. I could've said no. I knew what I was doing." He stood up and walked to the door, taking his coat and backpack off the hook on the wall. "See you later," he said.

Troy stood in the kitchen sipping from an enormous glass of ice water. "See you."

Lewis stepped outside into the cool morning air and took in a deep breath while he looked out over the foggy parking lot. He'd screwed up royally and lost the trust of a woman he cared about deeply. He had no idea how he was going to fix things between them, but he knew he had to try. One thing was for certain. He was never drinking again.

8

*B*ea rolled over and grabbed her phone from the bedside table. She didn't blame Meghan for sleeping on the sofa bed in the den, this bed was horrible. Bea couldn't wait to go to sleep in her own room, in her own bed tonight. But first, she'd have to get through this awful day.

She'd made a scene last night, letting her temper get the best of her. And although it had felt justified at the time, this morning it all seemed dumb.

Bea couldn't help but think that had she not gotten out of Lewis' car last night and instead had stuck around to talk things out with him, he wouldn't have felt the need to drink. She knew it wasn't her fault, per se, but that she could've made a better choice too.

She settled into the stiff pillows on the stiff bed and wrote her daily Reddit post on r/sober. Bea had never been the type to go to support group meetings, but she had a good therapist and she valued the sober community she'd found on Reddit.

Two years and twenty-one days sober. Alcohol free, but still letting my anger get the best of me. New boyfriend and I had a fight last night...

Bea laid out the entire problem in her post and then wrote at the bottom:

TL;DR: I broke up with my boyfriend because he was drinking and having fun without me. He isn't an alcoholic. What do I say to him? I don't know if I want to get back together or not.

She pulled the covers over her head and waited for the advice to come rolling in.

"Morning, Sunshine," Jamie said, coming into the room without knocking. "I come bearing caffeine."

"I'm trying to hide," Bea said from under the duvet.

She heard Jamie set a cup on the bedside table before he pulled the duvet off her head.

"Ughhhhhhhh," Bea said.

"Oh, whatever," Jamie said. "Just think, no matter how lousy you feel this morning, Lewis feels just as lousy *and* he has a hangover."

Bea stretched and sat up. "I've asked my fellow sobers what they think I should do," she said, reaching for the cup of coffee.

Jamie sat on the edge of the bed. "Good idea. You'll get no judgment from me no matter what. I'm Team Bea, always."

"Bea, do you want eggs?" Meghan called from the kitchen. "I'm making a dozen scrambled with cheddar."

"Yes, please," Bea said, nudging Jamie off the bed with her foot. "I totally get why you want to live here. The love of a woman who cooks non-stop, two greenhouses full of plants, a board game room. Chez Meghan is like Jamie paradise."

Jamie stood and grabbed Bea's hand, pulling her from the bed, careful not to make her spill her coffee. "For real, I'm super happy, Bea. I want that for you too."

"I'll get there," Bea said. "Eventually."

After breakfast, she showered and got dressed and Jamie drove her to work even though his shift wasn't until the afternoon. He pulled up in front of the Pinwheel instead of driving around to the rear parking lot.

"Just in case he's back there and you're not ready to see him yet," Jamie said, when she gave him a questioning look.

"Thanks," Bea said, unsure what she would've done if they had met Lewis in the parking lot. The image of her throwing herself into his open arms made her feel a lot better than the one where she ignored him, but there was still the slightest satisfaction in making him work for the embrace.

She got out of Jamie's car and went in through the front door which was already unlocked. Since Layla had become manager, the Pinwheel was open for business at nine on the dot, unlike the days when Avery would saunter groggily down the stairs from her apartment close-ish to ten.

"Morning," Layla said, brandishing a Swiffer duster from behind the front counter.

"Morning," Bea said, walking past her.

"I don't mean to be nosy," Layla said, "but I can't help but notice you sneaking in through the front door."

"You can't sneak in through the front door," Bea said, although, wasn't that what she was doing?

"Lewis have someplace else he has to be this morning?" Layla asked.

"No," Bea said. "We broke up." She headed to the back hall and hung up her things. Layla followed her.

"What happened?" Layla asked. "I thought things were going so well between you two."

Bea recounted the events of the night before. Each time she told it, both she and Lewis sounded more and more like two idiot peas in an idiot pod.

"Yikes," Layla said, hugging Bea's shoulders. "How many times do I have to tell people to leave the drama to me?"

"I promise I'll listen this time," Bea said. "Sober from alcohol, two years and twenty-one days. Sober from drama, seven hours."

Layla patted her on the back. "Okay, the timing for this is the worst, but I planned on having you set up the Valentine's Day display in the front window today."

Bea grinned. "You're trusting me to do a window display all by myself?"

"Yes," Layla said. "With Avery's and my final approval, of course."

The heaviness that was on her heart lightened some. Bea's love life may be a disaster, but her work life was looking up.

❧

*L*ewis dropped his backpack onto his table desk and took the clipboard off the wall. He hadn't seen Bea in the parking lot like he'd hoped to so he could start his epic apology tour, which made what he was about to do more difficult. Seeing her face and gauging how she felt about him would've bolstered his courage. But what needed to be done, needed to be done.

He approached Arthur's desk and hovered there a moment while his mentor finished squinting at a spreadsheet. Arthur pushed his glasses from the top of his head to his nose and looked up at Lewis.

"Criminy," Arthur said. "You look awful.

If you've got the flu, don't be a hero. Go home."

"I'm hungover," Lewis said. "I drank five glasses of the Imperial stout."

"Oh, boy," Arthur said. "That was dumb."

Lewis nodded. "Agreed."

"Did Bea give you a piece of her mind?"

"She broke up with me. Bea's been sober for two years and I... I screwed everything up."

"Yep. It sounds like you did. If I'd been around my wife after five glasses of the Imperial, she'd have taken me down a notch and then made me sleep out in my car without a pillow or blanket, just a beach towel for warmth."

"That's oddly specific," Lewis said.

"That," Arthur said, "is romantic relationships in your twenties."

"So, you understand where I'm coming from when I tell you I need to resign."

"What? No," Arthur said. "Pull a chair over here, you look like you're about to pass out."

Lewis dragged his bar chair over in front of Arthur's desk, sitting atop it, towering above his mentor, hugging the clipboard to his chest.

"Okay, not the chair I would've chosen, but you do you," Arthur said.

Lewis set the clipboard on Arthur's desk, rested his elbows on his knees and his head in his hands. "It's fine."

"Listen," Arthur said. "I get that you're willing to do anything to get your girl back, but you don't need to quit."

He flipped through a stack of papers and catalogs on his desk and pulled one out. "Pete and I were talking at the party the other night about expanding our line of craft sodas. The root beer and cream soda have been a hit with the family crowd, which is ultimately our target demographic. Mom and Dad can enjoy a house-brewed beer and a gourmet square, while the kids have a craft soda and a plain cheese or pep square."

Arthur folded open the catalog and handed it to Lewis. "I mentioned to Pete that this might be a good project for you to take on with your chemistry background and your willingness to learn new things. He agreed."

"You want me to brew soda?" Lewis

asked, scanning the ingredients in the catalog.

"Yes," Arthur said. "I want you to oversee the product line. There's demand for it even beyond what we could sell here. For instance, Small's has been after me for years to make a ginger beer to use in their Moscow mules. Customers love it when we can keep things as local as possible."

"I don't know what to say," Lewis said. "This is big, Art. Thank you for trusting me."

Arthur waved the comment away. "You've earned it." He grinned. "And since it's soda instead of beer, maybe that'll score you some points with your girl, huh?"

Lewis nodded. "It can only help."

"Great," Arthur said, picking up the clipboard. "Now please go home and sleep your hangover off, I can smell the stout sweating out of your pores. We can talk more about the sodas tomorrow."

Lewis tucked his chin and got a whiff of himself. *Never. Drinking. Again.* "I have a million ideas," he said, dragging his chair over to his table desk and stowing the catalog in his backpack.

Arthur grinned. "I knew you would," he

said, heading to the brewery. "See you tomorrow, kid."

"See you tomorrow."

Lewis left Mojo feeling like things were looking up. His love life was a disaster, but at least his work life was coming together.

9

*B*ea left Layla and Avery out front to critique her Valentine's Day window display, while she went into the meeting room to eat her lunch.

She scrolled through the sober Redditors' replies to the post she'd made that morning and ate the leftover pork loin and mashed potatoes Meghan had insisted Bea take with her.

An overwhelming number of the posts were positive and suggested that Bea give Lewis another chance. A few thought she should make him move out and be done with him forever.

Bea knew the decision was hers to make,

but it helped that most people agreed forgiving and asking for forgiveness were the way to go. That felt the most right to her. She finished her yummy lunch and then went back out on the shop floor.

"Well, done, Bea," Avery said. "What you did with the Bromelia balansae is fantastic."

"It's awesome," Layla said. "We wouldn't change a thing."

"Really?" Bea asked. "Thank you." The smile on her face went from wide to wider. "Um, since you're so pleased with me, now is probably a good time to ask for a favor."

"Ask away," Avery said.

"Can I have a snake plant to put in Lewis' office? It's pretty gray in there and could use some life."

"Of course," Avery said. "I'll help you pick one out. Were you thinking Sansevieria trifasciata Laurentii, Robusta, Moonshine..."

"Not Moonshine," Bea and Layla said at the same time.

"... Black Star, Gold Flame, Jade Star..." Avery said.

"Wait," Layla said, picking up an extra Bromelia balansae Bea hadn't used in her display. "What about a Heart of Flame? It's a fun way to say, 'sorry I'm such a hothead and will you still please kiss my face?'"

Bea grinned. "It's perfect."

"So I listed off all those Sansevieria trifasciata for nothing?" Avery asked, her hands on her hips.

"Oh, please," Layla said. "You loved every minute of it."

Avery snorted. "It's true."

Bea wrote a note on a small card saying what Layla had said about her being a hothead and explaining what the name of the plant was. Then she walked it over to Mojo's, knocking on the backdoor.

Lewis' mentor, Arthur stuck his head out. "Hey, there. If you're looking for Lewis, I sent him home for the day. He was in an awful way. Even tried to resign. Can you believe that?"

"He what?" Bea asked.

"This morning he came in here, looking like someone had shot his dog, and tried to resign," Arthur said.

"Did you let him?" Bea asked, her heart pounding. Was he leaving Braverton? Had she driven him away for good?

"Nah, I didn't let him. Instead I gave him

some good news, but he'll want to be the one to tell you all about it," Arthur said. He nodded at the plant. "You want me to put that on his desk?"

Bea handed the plant to Arthur. "Yes, thanks."

"Can I help you with anything else?" he asked.

"No," Bea said. "Just the plant."

Arthur smelled it. "Weird, but I like it. Nice colors. Have a good rest of your day."

"You too," Bea said. She returned to the Pinwheel and let herself in the back door.

"Did he like it?" Layla asked, from behind the counter where she was cutting lengths of cord for an upcoming macramé class.

Bea shook her head. "He wasn't there. His boss sent him home. He tried to resign this morning."

"Really?" Layla said. "That's extreme."

Bea started tearing up.

"Oh, honey," Layla said, coming around the counter to comfort her. "I'm sorry."

"I'm not crying because I'm sad," Bea said, her body racked with sobs. "What Lewis did was extreme but if he did it for me," she said, taking a stuttering breath. "He must really like me."

Layla threw her head back and laughed. "Forget like, Bea, I'd say this guy loves you."

Jamie came into the shop. "Hey, planty peop—" He stopped short. "Bea, are you okay? Why are you snotting all over Layla? Did something happen with Lewis?"

Layla filled him in while Bea composed herself.

"He is totally into you," Jamie said. "Wow, Bea, that's awesome." He furrowed his brow. "And it sort of explains the noises that were coming from your apartment."

"Huh?" Bea asked.

"I ran home to change and there was lots of loud banging. I was gonna be late or I would've checked it out. I just thought, I don't know, that maybe you were having the apartment divided in half or something."

"Because that's a likely explanation?" Layla asked, putting her hand on Jamie's forehead. "Are you sure you weren't having fever-induced hallucinations?"

Jamie shrugged. "Maybe pregnancy brain is contagious?"

"Layla," Bea said. "May I please have the afternoon off? I need to go home."

"Yeah you do," Layla said. "Jamie and I can hold down the fort and Avery's just upstairs if things get too busy."

"Jamie," Bea said. "I need your keys."

"They're in my coat pocket," Jamie said. "Don't worry about coming back for me. I'll walk over to OTG and catch a ride with the guys."

Bea squared her shoulders and walked toward the back hall. "Wish me luck," she said.

"Luck," Jamie and Layla called after her.

&a.

There *were* strange sounds coming from her apartment. Bea cautiously walked up the stairs, holding her house keys in a stabby manner just to be safe. She jiggled the doorknob, discovering it locked, so she knocked on the door.

Lewis answered it with his shirt off, his chest slick with sweat. When he saw her, he stepped forward, blocking the doorway so she couldn't see around him into the apartment.

"What are you doing home so early?" he asked, chuckling nervously.

Bea was certain she looked like a goof staring at his abs, but it was super difficult to pull her eyes away from the perfection. "Um," she said, looking up at him. "Jamie said it was loud." *Wow. Words were things.*

"I'm almost done," Lewis said, grabbing a hoodie from the hooks on the wall and putting it on. He came outside onto the landing and shut the door behind him before Bea could see what he was up to. "You can't go in there yet. It's a surprise."

"Okay," Bea said. "Does it have anything to do with what Arthur said you'd want to tell me?"

Lewis shook his head from side to side. "In a roundabout way."

"Why did you try to resign?" Bea asked. It was now or never.

Lewis brought his hand up to Bea's face and cupped it, stroking her cheek with his thumb. "I had a decision to make—you or the job. I chose you."

Bea felt the tears threatening to return. "You gave up your career and I brought you a plant," she said.

"What kind of plant?" Lewis asked. "One of those unkillable snake plants you mentioned?"

Bea shook her head. "A Heart of Flame," she said. "To apologize for being such a hothead last night."

Lewis brought his other hand up to Bea's face. "I like the fire in you," he said. "It keeps me in line and makes me want to be a better man."

Bea grabbed hold of his hoodie and pulled him closer, bringing her mouth up to meet his. Lewis kissed her softly, slowly, taking his time at first, moving from a low simmer to a rolling boil.

Bea eased her head back, her mouth swollen. "Are you sure I can't see my surprise now?"

Lewis smiled. "Ten minutes. Give me ten more minutes." He pointed toward the top of the stairs. "Sit there and don't peek. I promise it will be worth the wait."

Bea did as he asked, grateful her coat was long enough to protect her rear end from the cold, concrete stairs.

Nine minutes and fifty-two seconds later,

because of course she'd timed him, Lewis opened the door.

The first thing Bea noticed was that Lewis' couch was gone.

"I moved it into my room," he said. "This space is all about you."

The shelf that had been blocking the balcony door was replaced with a newly built one that arched over it instead, allowing them access to their small patio.

On the side of the slider that was fixed, Lewis had arranged all of Bea's hanging plants, so each had access to the bright, indirect light it craved. Down the legs of the arch were shelves at various heights, her potted plants tucked into them sorted by size and pot color. Along the top, Lewis had built three cubbies to hold her plant books, potting supplies, and her vintage vase collection.

"I confess I put all of the extra stuff up high so you'd need my help to get it down," he said. "Or a step stool, but I'd prefer if it were me."

"It's gorgeous," she said, bringing her hand to her mouth. Not only had he built the plant shelf, but he'd arranged the furniture so that her turntable and record collection were on display and not crammed into a corner behind her couch. "I love it."

Lewis cleared his throat. "I love you, Beatrix," he said. "I know it's early and you don't have to say it back, but it's true for me."

Bea slid her arms around his waist, and he embraced her, planting a kiss on top of her head.

"I love you, too," she said. "You're the best decision I've made in a long time." She pointed to her couch. "Now, let's sit. You're going to tell me all about this exciting thing at work."

They sat down and Lewis took Bea's left hand in his. "How would you feel about being the face of Mojo's newest craft soft drink, Trixie's Ginger Beer?"

Bea twisted a strand of her red hair around her right index finger and grinned. "I'm intrigued. Tell me more."

THE END

FREE BOOK!

Get a mailing list exclusive story when you sign up for the Write Free Press newsletter at www.writefreepress.com

Enjoy **Heart of Flame**? It would help me out tremendously if you would leave a short review wherever you purchased the book. As an indie author, word of mouth and written reviews are the best ways for new readers to discover me.

Pick up the next book in the Old Town Braverton Sweet Romance Series - *Bleeding Heart.*

Skye Perry and Lucas Lee each have their reasons for sneaking in through the back door of the Pinwheel Plant Shop to attend a macramé class.

Since her divorce, Skye goes nowhere without her dog, Rooster, and he's technically not allowed in the shop. Lucas (a.k.a. Lee Stone), well, he's a famous rock star lying low in Braverton until his stalker goes on trial in California.

When Lucas' therapist suggests he enroll in a crafty class to take his mind off his trauma, he waits until the last minute and is stuck taking macramé (whatever that is) in the suburbs. Lucas expects his classmates to be women of a certain age. Instead, he's pleasantly surprised to find himself tying knots with a cute dog trainer who has no idea who rocker Lee Stone is.

Skye would be perfectly fine hanging out in her studio apartment with Rooster or spending all her time at Girl's Best Friend— her dog adoption center specifically geared toward female identifying clientele. But her mom thought it was time she met some new humans and gave her a gift card to the Pinwheel for Christmas, so Skye signed up for a class. After Rooster falls asleep under Lucas' chair, Skye considers that maybe she was meant to meet just this one special human.

Falling hard and fast for one another, Lucas and Skye throw caution to the wind and go on a date in public even though they're risking the wrong people discovering where Lucas is.

When the inevitable happens, can the dog trainer and the rock star untangle themselves from their pasts to be together, or will they leave each other hanging?

ABOUT THE AUTHOR

Roxie Clarke writes sweet romances featuring houseplants, hunky heroes, and happily ever afters.

She lives outside Portland, OR with her husband and their five kids. It is loud at her house.

Catch up with Roxie at www.writefreepress.com

Special thanks to my beta readers S.S., S.N. and J.R. PN.

facebook.com/AuthorStacey

instagram.com/plantmom1975

pinterest.com/writefreepress

ALSO BY ROXIE CLARKE

CPSIA information can be obtained
at www.ICGtesting.com
Printed in the USA
BVHW082242290321
603655BV00003B/378